This book belongs to:

. . . .

For Nathaniel - GD.
For Mum, Dad and Michelle - AB

With special thanks (and apologies) to The Clash,
whose song 'London Calling' inspired the title of this book.
(In turn The Clash's title 'London Calling' came from the BBC World Service's
radio station identification: 'This is London calling...' used during World War II).

And Dr. Seuss, who inspired verse five, but as far as the author knows,
never actually visited London...

First published 2014 by order of the Tate Trustees by Tate Publishing,
a division of Tate Enterprises Ltd, Millbank, London SWIP 4RG
www.tate.org.uk/publishing

Text © Gabby Dawnay 2014. Illustrations © Alex Barrow 2014
Artwork by Paul Noble © Paul Noble 2014
All rights reserved.
A catalogue record for this book is available from the British Library
ISBN 978-1-84976-230-4

Distributed in the United States and Canada by ABRAMS, New York
Library of Congress Control Number applied for
Colour reproduction by Evergreen Colour Management Ltd, Hong Kong

LONDON CALLS!

GABBY DAWNAY ALEX BARROW

Tate Publishing

Big Ben is chiming; it's quarter to eight and

London is calling,  we mustn't be late...

We jump on a bus where an oyster's the fare

VISIT THE CROWN JEWELS

Marble Arch 159

and over the river to Parliament Square!

There are statues of lions and palaces fine;

there are parks packed with trees,

fancy restaurants to dine...

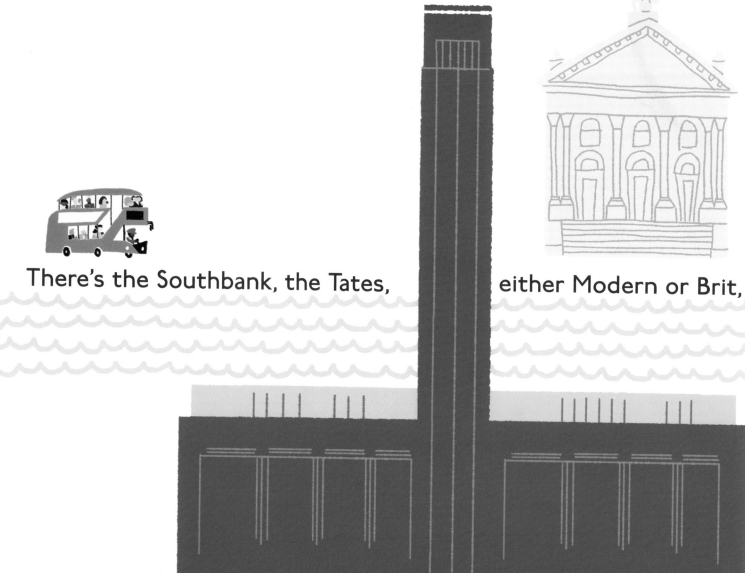

There's the Southbank, the Tates,   either Modern or Brit,

showing new art and old art and benches to sit...

There are shops selling shoes, there are shops selling socks,

£250.

£30

£40

there are shops selling fashionable dresses and clocks...

You can zoom on the tube, you can bicycle, scoot

You can talk as you walk, while the motorcars hoot!

There is concrete, graffiti and tower blocks high...

Spot the Gherkin and Shard  as they point to the sky!

SABRINA

There's a wheel with an Eye on a city that boasts

ancient towers and dungeons...

that shiver with ghosts

So many places and things to be seen...

from the column of Nelson to tea with the Queen...

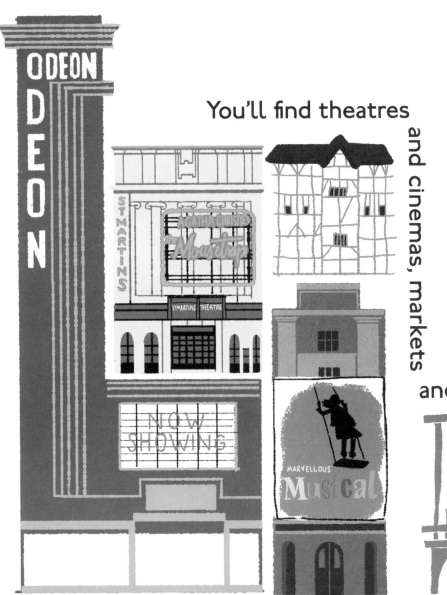

You'll find theatres

and cinemas, markets

and stalls

Oh you'd better listen when next London calls...

and supper is ready – we mustn't be late!

Meet Granny Rose and little Pearl

Hello! My name's Pearl and this is my Granny Rose. We're known as 'Pearlies' because our clothes are covered in pearl buttons!

Pearlies raise money for all sorts of good causes.

Thanks for coming on our whistle-stop tour of London – hope you enjoyed it! London is full of fantastic people and amazing places – there's so much to explore. Here are a few other things I bet you didn't know about this big, old, awesome city of ours. Over to you, Gran!

There are lots of funny names for buildings in London like The Gherkin, The Shard, Big Ben and The London Eye.

Can you spot them all in the pictures?

Did you know the saying 'The world is my oyster' comes from a play by William Shakespeare?

Is that why London travel cards are called Oysters?

Yes! I do love an oyster with a dash of Tabasco sauce. Scrummy! But they're pricey nowadays, mind... back in Shakespeare's day, oysters were as cheap as chips!

Was that back when you were a girl, Gran?

Steady on, Pearl, I'm not THAT old....

How many types of London transport can you spot in the book?

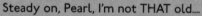

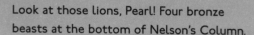
Look at those lions, Pearl! Four bronze beasts at the bottom of Nelson's Column.

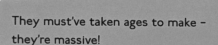
They must've taken ages to make – they're massive!

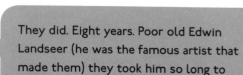
They did. Eight years. Poor old Edwin Landseer (he was the famous artist that made them) they took him so long to finish that everyone made fun of him.

That's mean! I love the statues all over London. Especially the Boy with a Dolphin, near my favourite bridge called... Gran, what's my favourite bridge called?

It's the Albert Bridge – one of the many bridges over the Thames. There are about 214 ways of crossing the river from start to finish, including all the big London bridges, the railway bridges, foot bridges and tunnels. That's a crossing for every mile!

Wow! So the Thames is...214 miles long?!

It is Pearl, it's the longest river in England. Londoners used to call it Old Father Thames because I suppose, it's such a long, old river running through the heart of London.

Did you know that seen from above, more than half of London is green or blue?

I'm not surprised! There are over 1,000 green spaces in London; not just parks, commons, heaths and public gardens, but garden squares, woods, city farms and cemeteries.

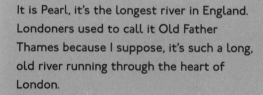

Do you have a favourite London park?

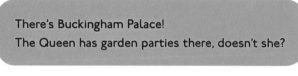
There's Buckingham Palace!
The Queen has garden parties there, doesn't she?

Yes, I've been to tea at the Palace.

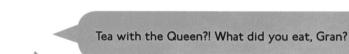
Tea with the Queen?! What did you eat, Gran?

Oh it was lovely, although I seem to remember the sandwiches being a bit on the small side. Let's see, we had...

Delicious!
What's your favourite food ever, Gran?

I like a good jellied eel!

Yuck! I like chips with loads of vinegar!
Do you think the Queen likes chips, Gran?
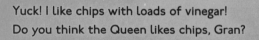

Come on Pearl,
let's go home for tea.

Can you spot Buckingham Palace in the book?

Buckingham Palace
TEATIME MENU

Earl Grey tea

accompanied by...
Honey and cream sponge cake
Chocolate biscuit cake
(Prince William's favourite)

Cucumber sandwiches
Smoked salmon sandwiches
(all crustless)

Jam pennies
(tiny raspberry jam sandwiches cut into circles the size of an old English penny)

Shall we get on the tube?

Why's it called the tube?

Because of the shape of the underground tunnels.

Oh I see! I like the whoosh of wind through the tunnel just before the train arrives – it's warm and stinky!

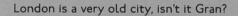

The tube is very old, too – the first bit was built 150 years ago. It's the oldest underground railway in the world!

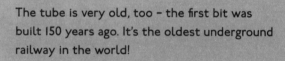

London is a very old city, isn't it Gran?

Yes, it is – but it's still growing and changing. It keeps me young, just like you do.

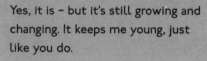